Jessica

by Kevin Henkes

PUFFIN BOOKS

HOLD ON TIGHT, JESSICA.

PUFFIN BOOKS
Published by the Penguin Group
A Division of Penguin Books USA Inc.
375 Hudson Street, New York, New York 10014
Penguin Books Ltd, 27 Wrights Lane, London W8 5TZ, England
Penguin Books Australia Ltd, Ringwood, Victoria, Australia
Penguin Books Canada Ltd, 10 Alcorn Avenue, Toronto, Ontario, Canada M4V 3B2
Penguin Books (N.Z.) Ltd, 182–190 Wairau Road, Auckland 10, New Zealand

Penguin Books Ltd, Registered Offices: Harmondsworth, Middlesex, England

First published in the United States of America by Greenwillow Books,
a division of William Morrow & Company, Inc., 1989
Reprinted by arrangement with William Morrow & Company, Inc.
Published in Picture Puffins, 1990
9   10   8

LIBRARY OF CONGRESS CATALOGING-IN-PUBLICATION DATA
Henkes, Kevin.   Jessica / by Kevin Henkes.   p.   cm.
Summary: Ruthie does everything with her imaginary friend Jessica;
then, on her first day at kindergarten, she meets a real new friend
with the same name.
ISBN 0-14-054194-2
[1. Imaginary playmates—Fiction.]   I. Title.
[PZ7.H389Je   1990]   [E]—dc20   89-36033

Printed in Hong Kong
Set in Monticello

GOOD JUMP,
/ JESSICA!

For
Annie
and
Geri and Mac

WE'RE ALMOST THERE, JESSICA.

JESSICA IS MY
BEST FRIEND.

Ruthie Simms didn't have a dog.
She didn't have a cat,
or a brother,
or a sister.
But Jessica was the next best thing.

Jessica went wherever Ruthie went.

To the moon,

to the playground,

to Ruthie's grandma's
for the weekend.

"There is no Jessica,"
said Ruthie's parents.

But there was.

She ate with Ruthie,

looked at books with Ruthie,

and took turns stacking
blocks with Ruthie,
building towers.

If Ruthie was mad, so was Jessica.

If Ruthie was sad,
Jessica was too.

And if Ruthie was glad,

Jessica felt exactly the same.

When Ruthie accidently
spilled some juice,
she said, "Jessica did it,
and she's sorry."

When Ruthie's parents called
a babysitter because they
wanted to go to a movie
one night, Ruthie said,
"Jessica has a stomachache
and wants you to stay home."

And when Ruthie turned five, it was
Jessica's fifth birthday too.

"There is no Jessica,"
said Ruthie's parents.

But there was.

SLEEP TIGHT, JESSICA.

She went to bed
with Ruthie,

RISE AND SHINE, JESSICA.

she got up with Ruthie,

READY OR NOT,
— HERE I COME,
JESSICA!

and she stayed with Ruthie
all the while in between.

On the night before the first day of
kindergarten, Ruthie's mother said,
"I think Jessica should stay home tomorrow."
Ruthie's father said, "You'll meet a lot
of nice children. You can make new friends."

But Jessica went anyway.

Jessica wanted to go home so badly that
Ruthie had to hold her hands and whisper
to her. When the teacher announced everyone's
name, Ruthie and Jessica weren't listening.

DON'T GET LOST, JESSICA.

Jessica crawled
through a tunnel
with Ruthie,

she took a nap
with Ruthie,

I CAN'T SLEEP EITHER, JESSICA.

and she shared
Ruthie's paintbrush
during art.

When all the children lined up two-by-two
to march to the lavatory, Jessica was
right next to Ruthie.

A girl came up to Ruthie and stood by her side. "Can I be your partner?" she asked. Ruthie didn't know what to say.

"My name is Jessica," said the girl.

"It *is*?" said Ruthie.

The girl nodded.

"Mine's Ruthie," said Ruthie, smiling.

And they walked down the hallway hand-in-hand.

Ruthie Simms didn't have a dog.
She didn't have a cat,
or a brother,
or a sister.
But Jessica was even better.

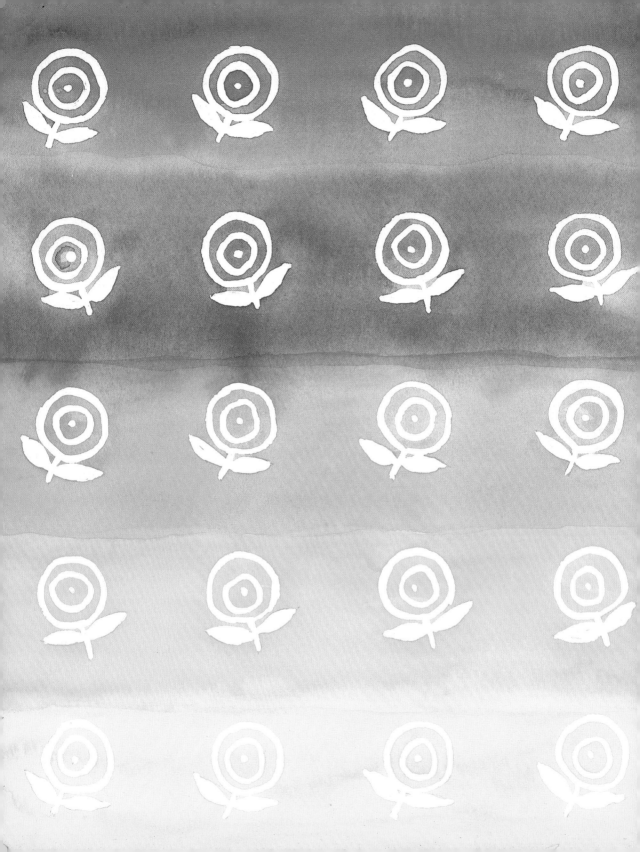